DATE DUE

OCT 1 6 1998	JUN 0 3 2003
NOV 2 7 1998	JUL 2 3 2004
JAN 0 1 1999	APR 2 8 2005
MAR 1 1999	SEP 3 1 2005
APR 1 6 1999	OCT 2 0 2005
MAY 0 7 1999	MAR 2 7 2006
MAY 1 4 1999	FEB 0 1 2007
MAY 2 7 1999	SEP 2 0 2007
SEP 1 3 1999	APR 2 8 2012
OCT 0 8 1999	JUN 2 5 2012
NOV 1 5 1999	AUG 1 7 2012
DEC 1 0 1999	
MAR 2 0 2000	
MAY 2 1 2000	
NOV 1 8 2000	
OCT 2 4 2002	

THE PiGS WENT MARCHiNG OUT!

written & illustrated by

Justin Rigamonti

LANDMARK EDITIONS, INC.

P.O. Box 270169 • 1402 Kansas Avenue • Kansas City, Missouri 64127
(816)241-4919

Dedicated to:
my mom and dad for
their love and encouragement;

and to God, my Heavenly Father,
for His love and care.

COPYRIGHT © 1998 BY JUSTIN RIGAMONTI

International Standard Book Number: 0-933849-70-2 (LIB.BDG.)

Library of Congress Cataloging-in-Publication Data
Rigamonti, Justin, 1979-
　　The pigs went marching out! /
written and illustrated by Justin Rigamonti.
　　p.　cm.
　　Summary: A dissatisfied pig encourages all the pigs to leave the
safety of their pigsty at Farmer Joe's to seek fun and thrills elsewhere,
only to return when they experience danger as well.
ISBN 0-933849-70-2 (lib.bdg. : alk. paper)
[1. Pigs—Fiction.　　　　2. Domestic animals—Fiction.
3. Stories in rhyme.]

I. Title.
PZ8.3.R453Pi　　1998
[E]—dc21
　　　　　　　　　　　　　　98-13553
　　　　　　　　　　　　　　CIP
　　　　　　　　　　　　　　AC

Creative Coordinator: David Melton
Editorial Coordinator: Nancy R. Thatch
Production Assistant: Brian Hubbard

Printed in the United States of America

Landmark Editions, Inc.
P.O. Box 270169
1402 Kansas Avenue
Kansas City, Missouri 64127
(816) 241-4919

Visit our Website — www.LandmarkEditions.com

THE PIGS WENT MARCHING OUT!

Some people think cartoon illustrations are easier to draw and much simpler to compose than are realistic illustrations. That is not true. Good cartoon illustrations may look easy and simple, but they also require a considerable amount of thought and skill.

In a good cartoon illustration, the characters are carefully designed, the compositions are planned, and the scenes are properly staged. The characters may be funny, but they are not silly. The humor is not thrown at the viewer. It is allowed to evolve naturally from the situations in the story.

Justin Rigamonti is a very good cartoon illustrator. His illustrations are thoughtfully developed. If they look easy and simple, it is because he has planned them so well and developed them with such skill.

Justin's characters are funny, and the situations in his story are funny. From the beginning there is no doubt that Pesky the Pig is the troublemaker. And there is no doubt that all the other pigs are his willing followers. We discover that Farmer Joe is indeed a kind man. And the dog he calls Riggs is...well...what can I say? He is a dog called Riggs.

Justin is a wonderful young man with whom to work. He is a good listener and he is open to suggestions. He always is willing to draw a scene from a different viewpoint and to make either major or minor adjustments. Even more important, he recognizes improvements when they are made.

The narrative poem in his book is both clever and witty. It does what a narrative poem should do — every line of every stanza moves the action and the story forward.

I think Justin has accomplished exactly what he set out to do. He has written and illustrated a thoroughly delightful and entertaining book.

To be delighted and entertained, all you have to do is turn the page.

— David Melton
Creative Coordinator
Landmark Editions, Inc.

There once was a farm, not too far away,
where the corn grew taller, day after day.
This farm was owned by a farmer named Joe —
the nicest farmer you'll ever know.

He cared for his crops. He cared for his creatures —
the mooers, the neighers, the cluckers, the screechers.
He cared for his wife and his hound dog called Riggs.
And he cared for his oinkers — all seventeen pigs.

Those pigs had life easy from morning till late.

They oinked and they oinked, they ate and they ate.

They loafed in the mud and lazed in the sun.

All were contented — all except one.

That pig was named Pesky. He was never pleased.

He grouched and he grumbled, he snorted and wheezed.

And early one morning, he sat in a pout,

thinking, "Now is the time for us pigs to march out!"

He stood up and called to all of his peers,
"Friends, pigs, countrymen, lend me your ears.
This mud hole is boring. This pigsty is dreary.
Let's get up and go to a place that is cheery.

"Let's go where there's fun and thrill after thrill,
where we can eat ice cream till we get our fill.
We can gobble down candy and caramel corn, too.
There'll be plenty for me and enough for you."

"Oh, that sounds like fun!" squealed all of the pigs.
"But what about Joe and the dog he calls Riggs?"
"Don't worry," said Pesky. "They're both out of sight.
They've gone hunting and won't be back till tonight.

"Come on!" ordered Pesky. "Don't linger about.
You pigs follow me! We're about to march out!"
So they all got up. They were ready for fun.
And those pigs marched out, one after one.

They marched past the barn. They marched past the house.

They marched past the cat who was chasing a mouse.

They marched past the cows who were swatting some flies.

They marched past the horses who neighed in surprise.

They marched past the chickens who stood in a row.

They marched past the rooster who started to crow.

They marched past a turkey who gobbled and gawked.

They marched past some crows who screeched and squawked.

They marched past a duck who stood near the road.
They marched past a turtle who sat by a toad.

They marched past a possum who hung upside down.
They marched and they marched till they came to a town.

All seventeen pigs were delighted to see
carnival rides and food that was free.
They gobbled down ice cream and big chocolate bars,
ate sweet cotton candy and strawberry stars.

The big roller coaster was the fastest of all!
The pigs were afraid they were going to fall!
And all those who liked to yell and to squeal,
took ride after ride on the high Ferris wheel.

They bumped each other in fast bumper cars,
guzzled down root beer and smoked big cigars.
Then one pig got sick, and right where he sat...
Well...it's probably best not to talk about that!

They rode all the rides and saw every sight.

They ate and they laughed from noon until night.

NIGHT?!! "Oh! No!" shouted Pesky. "Look at the sun!

It soon will be dark! Run fast, everyone!

"We've got to get home," he told all the pigs,
"before Farmer Joe and the dog he calls Riggs."
But they'd eaten so much, they were way overstuffed.
When they tried to run fast, they huffed and they puffed.

"There's a shortcut," said Pesky. "I'll show you the way."
And the pigs followed Pesky without a delay.
As they followed him up the steep mountain trails,
they shivered and shook from their heads to their tails.

Then the weather grew colder, and wouldn't you know,
the clouds opened up and it started to snow.
"Oh, no!" cried the pigs. "We're going to freeze!"
And soon the snow was up to their knees!

The pigs became angry. They started to shout,

"It's your fault, Pesky! You made us march out!"

But they kept on moving and tried to be brave.

Then one pig called out, "Oh, look, there's a cave!"

Those half-frozen pigs staggered right in,
not thinking whose home this cave might have been.
Like pink balls of yarn, they curled up to warm,
and they dreamed of their pigsty back on the farm.

But there was no time for sleeping or dreaming.
A ferocious growl made them wake up, screaming.
Then a horrible sight caused a terrible scare,
for into that cave came a BIG GRIZZLY BEAR!

The pigs squealed in terror and jumped all around.
They ran through the cave that went underground.
But the bear ran behind them. Oh, what a disaster!
And when he got close, they ran even faster.

Then they heard a loud BOOM! Could that be a shot?
The noise filled the cave and echoed a lot.

The footsteps came closer! There was nowhere to go...

But wait! That's no bear. It's someone they know!

When they saw Farmer Joe and the dog he called Riggs,
there were sighs of relief from all seventeen pigs.

"Where is that bear?" they wanted to know.

"He didn't stay long," smiled good Farmer Joe.

"'Cause when he saw Riggs and heard my loud gun,

that bear turned and high-tailed it out at a run.

"We were worried," said Joe as he looked all about.

"What made you pigs get up and march out?"

The pigs gave no answer. None even tried.

They just looked at Pesky who stood at the side.

"It's my fault," said Pesky. "There isn't a doubt.
I'm the one who got all these pigs to march out.
I didn't mean to be bad or cause any harm,
but I'm sure you won't want me back on the farm."

"Nonsense!" said Joe. "We're not angry at you.
You made a mistake, but all of us do.
You've taken the blame for what you did wrong.
Now let's all go home where we all belong."

Out of the cave went all seventeen pigs,
following Joe and the dog he called Riggs.
But none will forget from here and about
the day when the pigs went marching out!

BOOKS FOR STUDENTS BY STUDENTS

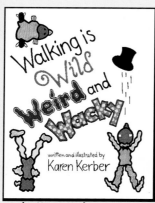

by Karen Kerber, age 12
St. Louis, Missouri
ISBN 0-933849-29-X   Full Color

by David McAdoo, age 14
Springfield, Missouri
ISBN 0-933849-23-0   Inside Duotone

by Amy Hagstrom, age 9
Portola, California
ISBN 0-933849-15-X   Full Color

by Isaac Whitlatch, age 11
Casper, Wyoming
ISBN 0-933849-16-8   Full Color

by Leslie Ann MacKeen, age 9
Winston-Salem, North Carolina
ISBN 0-933849-19-2   Full Color

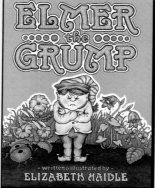

by Elizabeth Haidle, age 13
Beaverton, Oregon
ISBN 0-933849-20-6   Full Color

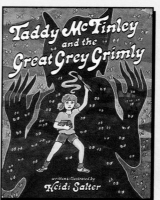

by Heidi Salter, age 19
Berkeley, California
ISBN 0-933849-21-4   Full Color

by Lauren Peters, age 7
Kansas City, Missouri
ISBN 0-933849-25-7   Full Color

by Aruna Chandrasekhar, age 9
Houston, Texas
ISBN 0-933849-33-8   Full Color

by Anika Thomas, age 13
Pittsburgh, Pennsylvania
ISBN 0-933849-34-6   Inside Two Colors

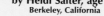

by Cara Reichel, age 15
Rome, Georgia
ISBN 0-933849-35-4   Inside Two Colors

by Jonathan Kahn, age 9
Richmond Heights, Ohio
ISBN 0-933849-36-2   Full Color

by Benjamin Kendall, age 7
State College, Pennsylvania
ISBN 0-933849-42-7   Full Color

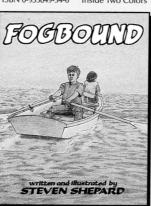

by Steven Shepard, age 13
Great Falls, Virginia
ISBN 0-933849-43-5   Full Color

by Travis Williams, age 16
Sardis, B.C., Canada
ISBN 0-933849-44-3   Inside Two Colors

by Dubravka Kolanović, age
Savannah, Georgia
ISBN 0-933849-45-1   Full Color

THE NATIONAL WRITTEN & ILLUSTRATED BY...AWARD WINNERS

by Dav Pilkey, age 19
Cleveland, Ohio
ISBN 0-933849-22-2   Full Color

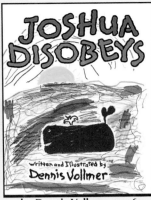

by Dennis Vollmer, age 6
Grove, Oklahoma
ISBN 0-933849-12-5   Full Color

by Lisa Gross, age 12
Santa Fe, New Mexico
ISBN 0-933849-13-3   Full Color

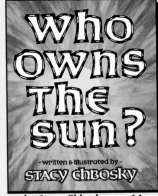

by Stacy Chbosky, age 14
Pittsburgh, Pennsylvania
ISBN 0-933849-14-1   Full Color

by Michael Cain, age 11
Annapolis, Maryland
ISBN 0-933849-26-5   Full Color

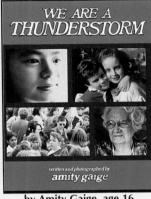

by Amity Gaige, age 16
Reading, Pennsylvania
ISBN 0-933849-27-3   Full Color

by Adam Moore, age 9
Broken Arrow, Oklahoma
ISBN 0-933849-24-9   Inside Duotone

by Michael Aushenker, age 19
Ithaca, New York
ISBN 0-933849-28-1   Full Color

by Jayna Miller, age 19
Zanesville, Ohio
ISBN 0-933849-37-0   Full Color

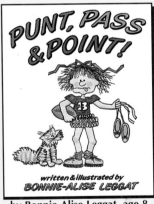

by Bonnie-Alise Leggat, age 8
Culpepper, Virginia
ISBN 0-933849-39-7   Full Color

by Lisa Kirsten Butenhoff, age 13
Woodbury, Minnesota
ISBN 0-933849-40-0   Full Color

by Jennifer Brady, age 17
Columbia, Missouri
ISBN 0-933849-41-9   Full Color

by Amy Jones, age 17
Shirley, Arkansas
ISBN 0-933849-46-X   Full Color

by Shintaro Maeda, age 8
Wichita, Kansas
ISBN 0-933849-51-6   Full Color

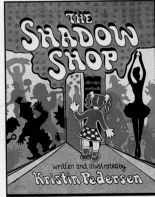

by Miles MacGregor, age 12
Phoenix, Arizona
ISBN 0-933849-52-4   Full Color

by Kristin Pedersen, age 18
Etobicoke, Ont., Canada
ISBN 0-933849-53-2   Full Color

Travis Williams
age 16

Anika D. Thomas
age 13

Isaac Whitlatch
age 11

Elizabeth Haidle
age 13

Miles MacGregor
age 12

Jayna Miller
age 19

Jonathan Kahn
age 9

Stacy Chbosky
age 14

David McAdoo
age 12

Amity Gaige
age 16